You Can't Lay an Egg If You're an Elephant

WRITTEN BY
Fred Ehrlich, M.D.

WITH PICTURES BY
Amanda Haley

🍎 BLUE APPLE BOOKS

To my mom with love
—A.H.

Text copyright © 2007 by Fred Ehrlich
Illustrations copyright © 2007 by Amanda Haley
CIP Data is available.
Published in the United States 2007 by
🍎 Blue Apple Books
P.O. Box 1380, Maplewood, N.J. 07040
www.blueapplebooks.com
Distributed in the U.S. by Chronicle Books

First Edition
Printed in China
ISBN 13: 978-1-59354-606-9
ISBN 10: 1-59354-606-8

1 3 5 7 9 10 8 6 4 2

Table of Contents

INTRODUCTION

An elephant egg?
Don't be absurd!
If you want an egg,
Go find a bird.

All animals must have babies that will grow up to be like them. If they didn't, there would be no more elephants or birds or butterflies or baboons or people. Every animal would become extinct.

When an animal has a baby, it is reproducing itself. Animals reproduce themselves in different ways. One way is by laying eggs. The new baby grows inside the egg until it hatches.

Animals that lay eggs are called oviparous (oh-VIP-uh-russ).

I'm OVIPAROUS.
I'm a red hen named Meg.
Why am I clucking?
I just laid an egg!

4

Other baby animals grow inside their mothers' bodies. Animals that carry their babies inside their bodies before the babies are born are called viviparous (vie-VIP-uh-russ).

I am VIVIPAROUS!
I began inside my mother
With four other kittens—
Three sisters and one brother.

It's easy to tell when a woman is having a baby—her belly gets bigger, and bigger, and bigger. After nine months, her baby is born.

I can't remember
The day I was born,
The 5th of September
At 8 in the morn.

I must have been there.
I had to be.
'Cause if I wasn't,
I wouldn't be me.

CHAPTER ONE

Small Birds

Birds come in different sizes, and so do their eggs. A hummingbird egg is as small as a blueberry. An ostrich egg is as big as a grapefruit.

Bird eggs come in different colors too. Some eggs are plain white, or brown, or blue. Others are multi-colored.

I'm inside an egg
That's colored pale blue.
When I come out
Will I be blue, too?

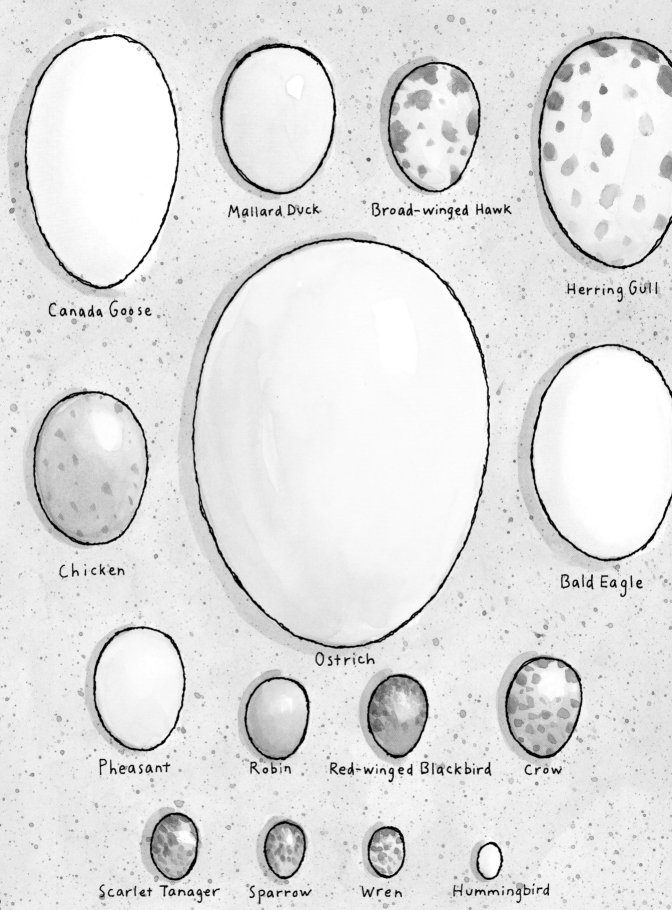

Canada Goose

Mallard Duck

Broad-winged Hawk

Herring Gull

Chicken

Ostrich

Bald Eagle

Pheasant

Robin

Red-winged Blackbird

Crow

Scarlet Tanager

Sparrow

Wren

Hummingbird

ROBINS

Robin eggs are a pretty pale blue.

Robins sit on their eggs for about two weeks before the eggs hatch. The new chicks are helpless. Their eyes are closed. They can hardly move. Their parents must bring food to them.

But baby robins grow up fast. In just two weeks, they are ready to fly. But even after the baby birds have grown almost as big as their parents and can get their own food, they still beg their parents to feed them.

I laid your egg and kept it warm
Until you hatched. In a storm,
I spread my wings to keep you dry.
Then I taught you how to fly.

I've fed you countless worms and bugs,
Grasshoppers, seeds, beetles, slugs.
But now you are as big as me—
Go feed yourself and let me be!

HUMMINGBIRDS

All eggs must be kept warm in order for the chick inside to grow. Some bird parents take turns sitting on their eggs. But not the hummingbird.

Mother hummingbird does the job all by herself. When the air is cold, she will sit right on the egg. But when it is hot, she will stand over the egg and keep it cool with her shadow. When she needs to change position, she flies a few inches straight up in the air, turns around, then comes back down.

A hummingbird nest is a tiny one-inch cup attached to a twig with spider silk. As many as three baby birds live inside. The mother gathers nectar from flowers, then squirts it down her babies' throats.

**Hummingbird chicks,
Open wide
So Mom can squirt
Your food inside.**

CHICKENS

Chicken eggs take about 21 days to hatch. Like other birds, the chick has to crack its way out of the egg. To do this, each chick has a hard, sharp "tooth" on its beak called an egg tooth. After the chick has hatched, the egg tooth falls off.

It's crowded in here!
I can't move my wing.
And it's so dark,
I can't see a thing.

Peck, little chick.
You'll get out by-and-by.
Just use your egg tooth
And you'll soon see the sky.

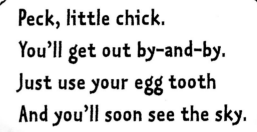

CHAPTER TWO

Large Birds

OSTRICHES

The bigger the bird, the bigger the egg. The largest egg is laid by an ostrich. Each ostrich egg weighs almost 3 1/2 pounds! An ostrich father sits on the nest, which is simply a hole scratched into the sand. He lays his long neck on the ground so that his body looks like just another small hill.

After about 6 weeks, the baby ostriches hatch. By then they are able to eat on their own. In the first five months of their lives, they will grow one foot each month. When they are fully grown they can stand 7 to 9 feet tall and weigh from 200 to 350 pounds.

Ostriches cannot fly, but they are great runners. They are the fastest 2-legged animal on earth, reaching speeds of up to 45 miles per hour.

PENGUINS

Penguins cannot fly. Their wings are like flippers, so they swim. They can spend months in the ocean without ever going on land. But they cannot stay underwater like fish. They must come to the surface to breathe. And they must come onto land to lay their eggs and hatch their young.

Penguins live only in the southern hemisphere, mostly in Antarctica near the South Pole.

The largest penguin is the EMPEROR PENGUIN. It can grow up to four feet tall and weigh up to 95 pounds. Female emperor penguins lay one large egg a year.

The penguins walk about seventy miles over ice and snow from the ocean to the place where they will lay their eggs. Since the only place they can get food is in the ocean, they must now go for weeks without eating.

If the egg slips away as the parents try to transfer it, it freezes and there will be no chick.

After a mother penguin has laid her egg, she is near to starving. It has taken a lot of energy to make the egg. She has lost almost a third of her weight. She needs to eat. So she transfers the egg onto the father's feet. Then she returns to the ocean to feed.

The father covers the egg with a flap of skin hanging from his belly. In about two months, while its mother is away, the chick will hatch.

After some time, the mother returns, fat and well fed. The father transfers the chick back to its mother. Now the chick can get its first meal. The mother regurgitates (throws up) food from her stomach and feeds it to her baby.

Now it is the father's turn to feed. Back to the ocean he goes. While he is gone, the chick will eat and grow and take its first steps. Then its mother will go back to the ocean to eat, leaving the chick alone until the father returns.

Back and forth, back and forth. One parent leaves to eat while the other stays to feed and protect the chick. But at least the trip gets shorter as spring, then summer, comes to the Antarctic and melts the ice.

Finally, both parents return to the sea. The chicks are left behind. Most of them will never see their parents again. But a few weeks later, the chicks too will dive into the ocean. They will stay there for four years. Then, in the fifth year, they will return to the place where they were born to lay their eggs and care for their babies.

Down through a hole in the ice
Penguins dive into the sea.
They swim in water that's too cold
For either you or me.

CHAPTER THREE

Small Mammals

Mammals are vertebrates—animals with backbones. They feed their young with milk. They are warm-blooded, which means that their body temperature does not change when it's cold or hot outside.

Most mammals do not lay eggs. The mothers carry their young inside their bodies in a special place called a womb or uterus.

MICE

Mice are among the smallest mammals. They have all the same equipment inside their bodies that large mammals like elephants and whales have. They give birth to live young, then feed and protect them until they are able to take care of themselves and have babies of their own.

Mice are only four inches long, but they can produce a startling number of baby mice. A female mouse gives birth to four to eight babies at a time. She can have four to six litters each year. So, in one year, one female mouse could have forty-eight babies.

A mouse can live for up to four years. So, in her lifetime, one female mouse could give birth to 192 babies!

I built a house
For me and my spouse.
I didn't know
That my house had a mouse.

The mouse in my house
Got himself a spouse.
So now my house
Had me and a spouse,
And a mouse and a spouse.

We wanted a child
My spouse and I.
We had a baby
By and by.
The mouse and his spouse
Raised a family too.
They had two hundred babies—
We had two!

Those babies found spouses
And set up mouse houses
All over our house.
Their mouse families grew.
But my spouse and I
Decided what to do.
We left our house
To the mouse and his spouse
And to one thousand mice.
Now aren't we nice?

DOGS

Female dogs are pregnant for about two months, and their litters can be anywhere from two to sixteen pups. At birth the pups are blind and just strong enough to crawl to their mother's teats and nurse.

Pups open their eyes after ten days and are able to walk after twenty. By one month they have all their milk teeth. The milk teeth are very sharp as anyone who has raised puppies can tell you.

PLATYPUS

The platypus is part of a small group of mammals called monotremes. Like other mammals, the platypus nurses its newborn babies with milk. But unlike other mammals, the platypus lays eggs.

After laying her eggs, the female platypus curls her body around them to incubate them (keep them warm) until the babies hatch. After they hatch, the babies will rely on their mother's milk for three to four months before leaving their nest and finding food for themselves.

There are only three species of monotremes in the world today: the platypus and two kinds of spiny anteaters.

Monotreme

Two spiny anteaters made a fuss
When they ran into a platypus.

They said, "Our rarity is quite extreme.
We're egg-laying, mammalian monotremes!"

The platypus answered, "Well, I'm one, too.
Pleased to meet you. How do you do?"

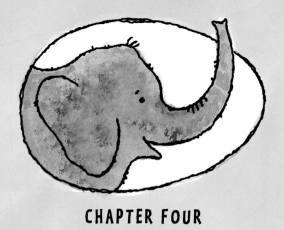

Large Mammals

ELEPHANTS

African elephants are the largest land animals. A mature male can weigh 7 tons (that's 14,000 pounds) and stand more than 12 feet high.

A female elephant is pregnant longer than any other mammal on earth—for 18-22 months. She usually gives birth to just one baby. When it is born, her baby will weigh from 170 to 300 pounds. It will drink 3 gallons of its mother's milk every day.

Elephants can live up to 80 years. During her lifetime, a female elephant can give birth to 7 or 8 babies, but this rarely happens.

BLUE WHALES

Blue whales are the largest animals in the world. A big blue whale can grow up to 110 feet long and weigh more than 160 tons. That's 320,000 pounds, or more than 22 large male African elephants!

Blue whale mothers are pregnant for 10-12 months. When it is born, the new whale pup will be about 23 feet long. Its mother's milk is very rich in fat, so the baby grows quickly. By the time it is seven months old, it will be 52 feet long. By twelve months it will weigh about 26 tons.

All that milk helps the baby grow a thick layer of fat, called blubber, to protect it from the cold sea. The whale's life is spent entirely in the ocean.

Whales breathe air, so they have to come to the surface to blow out old air (called spouting) and breathe in fresh air. Whale pups do this from the time they are born.

If I were a whale,
Living under the sea,
You'd need a submarine
To travel with me!

CHIMPANZEES

Chimpanzees are like humans in many ways. If you described a chimp, someone might think you were talking about a human being.

RIDDLE

I was born after a nine-month pregnancy and soon began to nurse. I soon became alert and curious. I like to play and be with others. In groups, I chatter a lot. I am good at solving problems like finding ways to get food that is out of reach. Who am I?

Of all the animals in the world, chimpanzees are the most like humans. Chimpanzees create families that last a lifetime. They use facial expressions, body language, and vocalizations to communicate with other chimps. When chimpanzees meet after being apart, they may kiss, hug, or pat each other. Chimps tickle their children, hold hands, or shake their fists much as we do.

Answer: baby chimp   baby human
Both answers are correct.

Of course, the differences between people and chimps are obvious. Chimps never learn to speak, write, or draw pictures of what they see. They do, however, show feelings of anger, fear, surprise, disgust, and sadness. They can't tell us in spoken words what they are feeling, but their faces and bodies tell a lot.

A scientist raised his 10-month-old son and a 7 ½-month-old chimp together. He treated them alike. At first the chimp was quicker to understand commands such as "Come here" or "Sit down." She was also stronger and better at handling things.

After a few months, the boy was able to understand more complicated instructions and began to solve problems that were too difficult for the chimp.

How would my life be
As a chimpanzee?
I could ride
on my mommy's back
And eat bananas
For my snack.
I'd sleep in a nest
High in a tree—
Deep in the forest
I'm a chimpanzee!

CHAPTER FIVE

Comparing Human and Chimp Babies

It takes nine months of growing inside the mother's body before a human baby is ready to live in the outside world. It takes nine months for a chimp baby too.

Human newborns can breathe to get oxygen and suck to get food. They can also open their eyes, cry, hiccup, sneeze, cough, pee and poop, and sleep. But they can't take care of themselves.

Exactly the same things are true of chimpanzee newborns.

NEWBORN

Chimpanzee

Newborn chimpanzees are with their mothers all the time. Their mothers hold them, but they can also cling to their mothers' bellies by themselves. They use their feet as well as their hands to hold on so that their mothers are free to move around. The mothers won't let any other chimp touch her baby except for its own siblings.

Child

Newborn humans have to be held to nurse or take a bottle or to be moved around. They are with their mothers or other adults some of the time, but they are usually put down to sleep. Human mothers usually let other people hold their babies.

TWO MONTHS

Chimpanzee

The baby chimp begins to suck its thumb and reach toward objects. It can now stand upright if holding onto its mother.

Child

At this age the infant human is able to hold up its head. It begins to smile when a familiar person approaches and talks to it. It can't get in trouble like the chimp infant because it can't even turn over.

SIX MONTHS

Chimpanzee

The chimp is now riding on its mother's back. It has taken its first steps and begun to climb up saplings or branches. It plays with its mother and laughs when it is tickled, and it has learned to kiss.

Child

By six months the human baby can turn over and sit up. It can also laugh and have fun when people play games.

TWO YEARS

Chimpanzee

By now the young chimp is playing at attacking—running at another baby and hitting—and nest-building. It has also learned to comfort and groom another chimp. Grooming—cleaning another chimp's fur—is an important chimp behavior. It keeps the chimps clean and comforts them.

Child

At two years, children can talk well enough to explain what they want. They can run and climb, listen to stories, and play simple games. They fuss and cry but can usually be comforted and reasoned with.

31

Chimpanzee

The young chimp, now beginning to lose its baby teeth, starts to move around for short periods without its mother.

Child

By six years, children can do the most important things they will need for the rest of their lives. They can talk well and understand most of what they are told. They can start learning to read, write, and do arithmetic. They can usually stay out of trouble and danger though adults are needed for guidance and protection.

Animals do many things that we can't do. But we can do things that no animal can do. We can talk and tell our children about what happened in the past. We can think about the future. We can write about what happened yesterday or a thousand years ago. Our brains allow us to think, feel, and respond to the world around us in far more complicated ways than other animals can.

But whether an animal hatches out of an egg or comes out of its mother, a baby has to grow and learn a lot before it is a grown-up chicken or ostrich or elephant or chimpanzee or human being.

Cats give birth to kittens.
Bees produce more bees.
Dogs give birth to pups.
Acorns fall from trees.

Whales cannot lay eggs.
Kids do not have wings.
The world we have is made
Up of expectable things.

" B"